One Snail and ME

A Book of Numbers and Animals and a Bathtub

by Emilie Warren McLeod | *Illustrated by* Walter Lorraine

An Atlantic Monthly Press Book Boston · *Little, Brown and Company* · Toronto

 LIBRARY OF CONGRESS CATALOG CARD NO. 61-5333. *Ninth Printing* ATLANTIC-LITTLE, BROWN BOOKS ARE PUBLISHED BY LITTLE, BROWN AND COMPANY IN ASSOCIATION WITH THE ATLANTIC MONTHLY PRESS. *Published simultaneously in Canada by Little, Brown & Company (Canada) Limited.* PRINTED IN THE UNITED STATES OF AMERICA.

Books by

EMILIE WARREN McLEOD

The Seven Remarkable Bears

Clancy's Witch

One Snail and Me

To my grandmother "SBW," and her eight great-grandchildren

There are things to do alone in a tub,

like being a fish and being a boat,

like bubbling and sloshing and chasing soap.

But it would be ever so much more fun

if done

by two or three or four.

Two whats?

Three whats?

Four or more whats?

Well, I do have a snail.

1 snail

makes a beautiful,

bubbly, silvery trail

on the edge of the tub.

And turtles, I have

2 turtles,

so bashful they won't leave their homes.

They blink and promise not to tell

that I am here without my shell.

One snail,

and me.

I have **3** ducks,

three Peking ducks.

They quack in mandarin Chinese

and swim with busy orange feet

around the island of my knees.

Two turtles,

one snail,

and me.

Better yet, I have

4 seals,

who juggle my soap on the tips of their tails

while unpacking the lunch

they brought in tin pails,

for three ducks,

two turtles,

one snail,

and me.

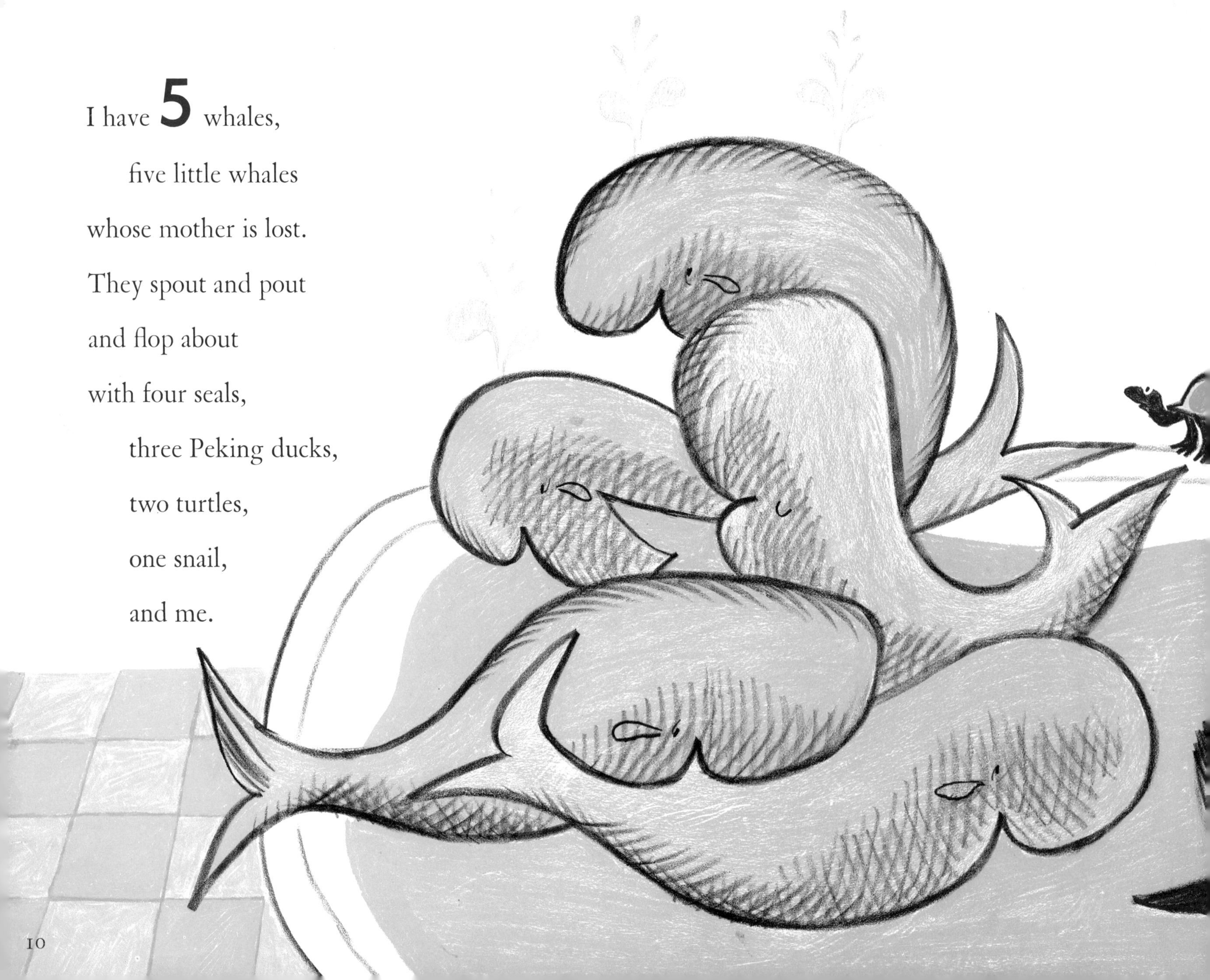

I have **5** whales,

five little whales

whose mother is lost.

They spout and pout

and flop about

with four seals,

three Peking ducks,

two turtles,

one snail,

and me.

SOAP

And that's not all.

I have **6** kangaroos,

six girl kangaroos,

with a pocket each

filled with sand for a beach

and with red-striped umbrellas and bathing shoes

for five little whales,

four seals,

three Peking ducks,

two turtles,

one snail,

and me.

I have **7** bears,

seven hungry bears.

They float on empty honey jars

while eating sticky candy bars

which they are very glad to share

with six kangaroos,

five small whales,

four seals,

three Peking ducks,

two turtles,

one snail,

and me.

And **8** alligators,

eight little alligators,

because the bigger ones

are people eaters

and we're not fond of them at all–

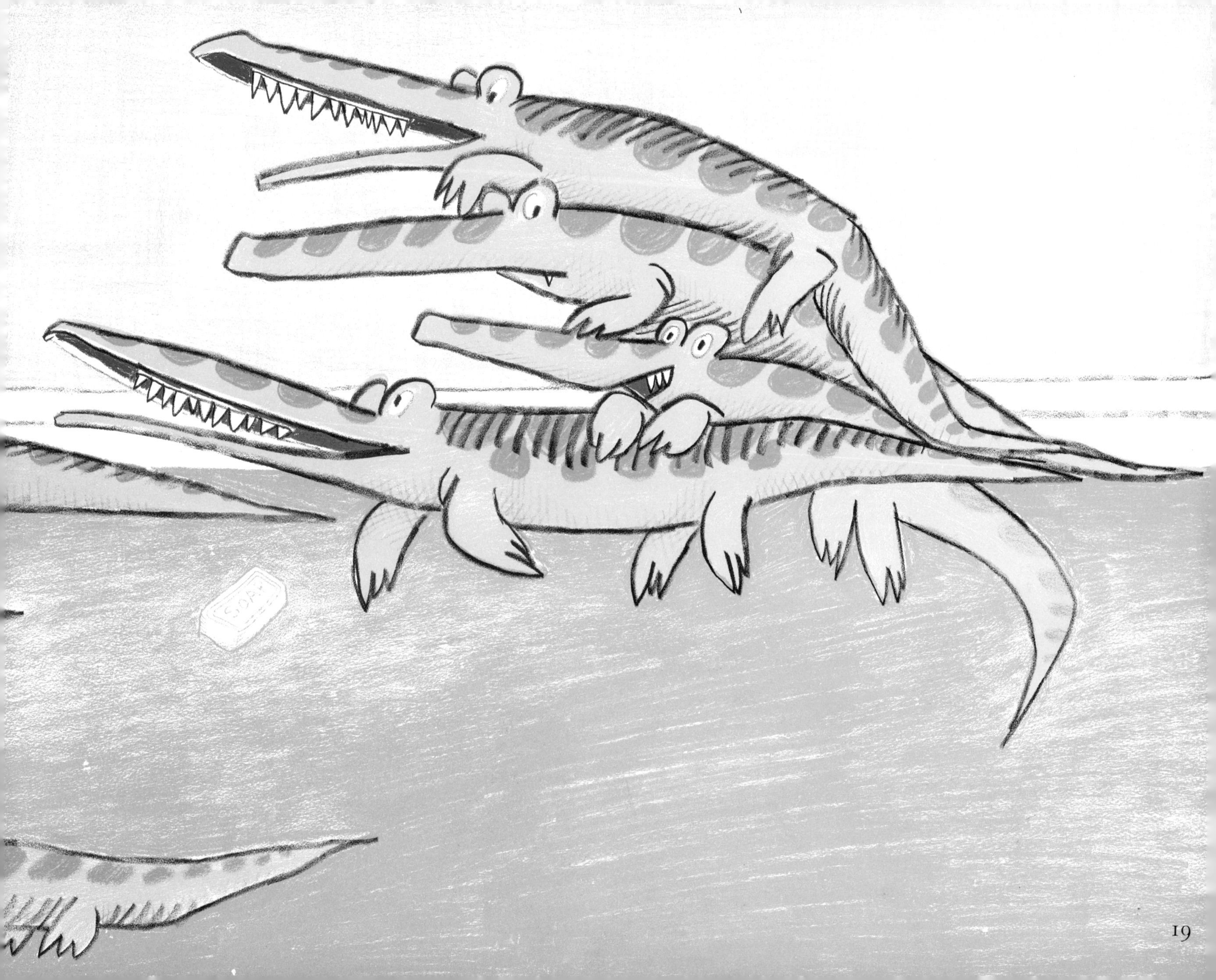

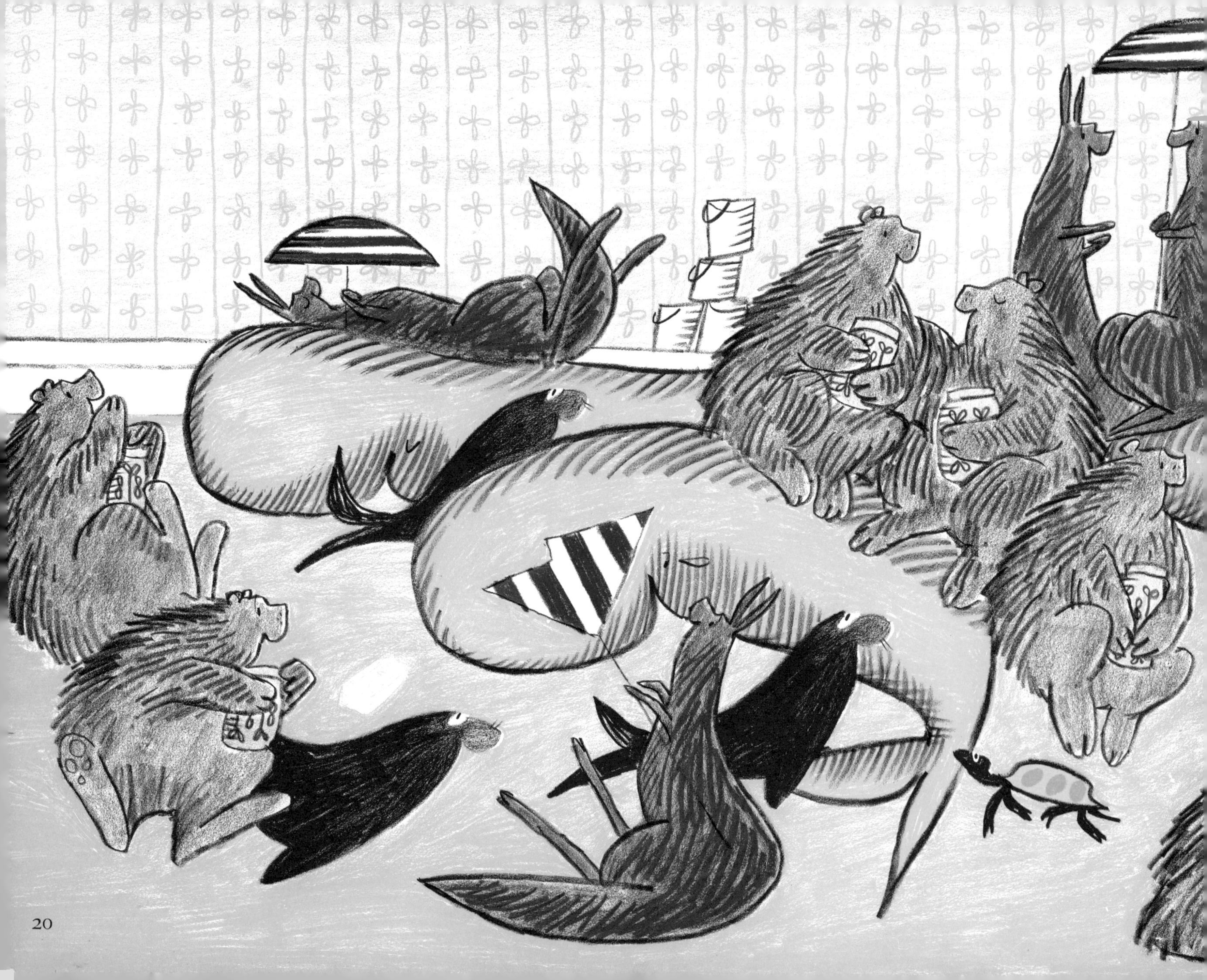

the seven hungry honey bears,

six kangaroos,

five small whales,

four seals,

three ducks,

two turtles,

one snail,

and me.

I have **9** hippopotamuses–

or nine fine hippopotami–

of such tremendous heft

they take up all the tub that's left,

with most of them outside;

and eight alligators,

seven hungry bears,

six kangaroos,

five whales,

four seals,

three ducks,

two turtles,

one snail,

and me.

I have **10** little minnows who tickle,

ten little minnows

with prickly fins,

who wriggle, and squiggle,

and tickle

the nine hippopotamuses,

eight alligators,

seven bears,

six kangaroos,

five whales,

four seals,

three ducks,

two turtles,

one snail,

and me.

We're all of a jumble
of splashes and bubbles,
of bathing shoes, beach sand,
of honey jars, lunch, and
giggles and tickles,
of water and soap.
We're all of a jumble
  of me,
  one snail,
  two bashful turtles,
  three Peking ducks,
  four seals with lunch in pails,
  five little whales,

six kangaroos with bathing shoes,

seven hungry bears,

eight alligators,

nine fine hippopotamuses,

and ten little minnows who tickle.